TIME
FOR KIDS
READERS

The Star-Spangled Banner

by Lisa deMauro

Harcourt

Orlando   Austin   Chicago   New York   Toronto   London   San Diego

Visit *The Learning Site!*
www.harcourtschool.com

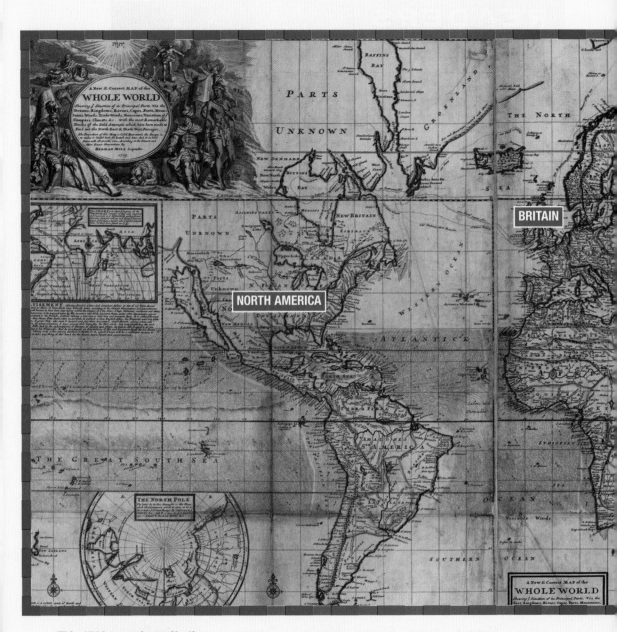

This 1719 map shows North America and Britain.

Start with a war between a young country and its previous rulers. Take one lawyer who likes to write poems in his spare time. Give the lawyer a front-row seat at a big battle. Add the tune of a popular song and a giant flag. What do you get? The ingredients for "The Star-Spangled Banner"!

"The Star-Spangled Banner" is the national anthem—or song—of the United States. You may know most or all of the words to our national anthem. But do you know what they mean? Do you know the story behind the anthem?

To understand the story of "The Star-Spangled Banner," you first have to go back to the early years of the United States. The American Revolution ended in 1783. Afterward, the United States was an independent nation. It was no longer a group of colonies that belonged to Britain.

The American Revolution was over, but the angry feelings were still there. The British were unhappy that the colonies had won the war. The powerful former rulers refused to believe that the young country would last. The British still held land in Canada and many people in the U.S. hoped to force them out of there as well. That way the Canadian land could become part of the United States. This would show Britain that the United States was a strong country.

For all these reasons, feelings remained bad between the United States and Britain. Many people in the U.S. wanted to fight the British again. The War of 1812 was the result.

The armies of Britain and the U.S. battled for about two years. Neither side seemed to be winning. Then in August of 1814, British troops marched into Washington, D.C. They quickly headed for the White House! The first lady, Dolley Madison, was about to have a dinner party. She heard that the British soldiers were on their way. As she left for a safer place, she took some valuable items with her. One was a painting of George Washington.

When the British soldiers arrived at the White House, they found Dolley's hot meal on the dining table. They sat down and ate it! When they finished, they burned the White House. They also burned the Capitol and other government buildings.

This painting shows what the White House
might have looked like in 1814.

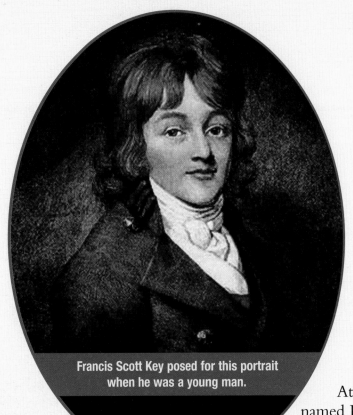
Francis Scott Key posed for this portrait when he was a young man.

At the same time, a man named Dr. William Beanes was taken prisoner by British troops. The British took their prisoner on board a ship in the Chesapeake Bay. When news spread of Dr. Beanes's capture, many people were upset. Fearing he might be harmed, his friends asked a young lawyer to try to get Beanes released. That lawyer's name was Francis Scott Key.

Key and Colonel John Skinner, whose job it was to help arrange prisoner exchanges in war, set sail together from Baltimore. They wanted to find the British fleet in Chesapeake Bay. They convinced the British to release Dr. Beanes. However the British were ready for their next attack.

Since the British navy had aimed its guns at Fort McHenry in Baltimore, naval officials were afraid Beanes and his rescuers would warn the U.S. forces of the attack. So Key, Skinner, and Beanes were "invited" to stay aboard the British ship. From there, they could watch the battle take place. They could also see the United States flag flying over the fort.

Francis Scott Key, aboard a British ship, looks toward Fort McHenry.

Major George Armistead ordered
two flags for Fort McHenry.

In 1813 Major George Armistead, the commander of Fort McHenry, ordered two flags from a flagmaker in Baltimore. He said he wanted one of the flags to be extra large so that "the British would have no trouble seeing it from a distance." It was huge—30 feet (9 m) high and 42 feet (13 m) long! Its stars were 2 feet (less than 1 m) across! The fort also had a second, smaller flag, called a *storm flag*. It was made to fly above the fort in bad weather. It measured 17 feet (5 m) by 25 feet (8 m).

Mary Pickersgill sewed the Star-Spangled Banner and the storm flag.

The flagmaker was Mary Pickersgill. Pickersgill could not lay out the large flag in her home. She had to find a big room to spread out the flag on a floor, so she could see where to place the stars. The whole flag was stitched by hand.

These flags were made at the time when the United States was adding one star and one stripe for each state that joined the Union. So, the flags each had 15 stars. They also had eight red and seven white stripes.

People must have realized that it would not work to keep adding stripes to the flag. In 1818 the U.S. Congress passed a law that all future flags would have only 13 stripes. That was one for each of the 13 original states. A new star would be added for each new state. If Congress had not changed the rule, we would have a very striped flag today!

On the morning of September 13, 1814, the British attacked Fort McHenry. For 25 hours, bombshells roared from the British guns. The air was thick with smoke. The sound of exploding rockets was deafening. By evening, it was raining.

Meanwhile, Key stood watching from the water. He stared into the smoky, wet night. As long as the attack was going on, the fort must still be under U.S. control. Then, in the early morning darkness, all was quiet. What did it mean? Had the fort surrendered? Or had the British given up the attack? Key and his friends waited and watched. With the first light of dawn, they understood: The "Star-Spangled Banner" had been raised!

Fort McHenry is shown under attack.

Key felt a great sense of joy and relief. He wanted to put his feelings into words. He pulled a letter from his pocket. On its back, he began to write a poem about the battle. Several days later, in a hotel room in Baltimore, Key reworked his poem. He named it "Defence of Fort M'Henry." He showed the poem to his brother-in-law, who suggested that Key publish it. They made copies at a newspaper office. The copies were given out to the soldiers at Fort McHenry and the citizens of Baltimore. The poem was renamed "The Star-Spangled Banner."

Where did the music come from? It was an English song popular in the United States called "To Anacreon in Heaven." Years earlier, Francis Scott Key had written another poem that he set to the same tune. Key had that song in mind when he wrote the "The Star-Spangled Banner." His words fit the music perfectly. When he published the song, he set it to that music.

The song was reprinted in U.S. newspapers. It quickly became popular. In December 1814 the war ended. By then the song was being played throughout the United States.

The Star-Spangled banner.

O! say, can ye see by the dawn's early light
What so proudly we hail'd by the twilight's last gleaming?
Whose bright stars & broad stripes, through the clouds of the fight,
O'er the ramparts we watch'd were so gallantly streaming?
And the rocket's red glare, the bomb bursting in air,
Gave proof through the night that our flag was still there.
O! say does that star-spangled banner yet wave
O'er the land of the free & the home of the brave?

On that shore, dimly seen through the mists of the deep,
Where the foe's haughty host in dread silence reposes,
What is that which the breeze, o'er the towering steep,
As it fitfully blows, half conceals, half discloses?
Now it catches the gleam of the morning's first beam,
In full glory reflected, now shines on the stream.
'Tis the star-spangled banner—O! long may it wave
O'er the land of the free & the home of the brave.

And where is that host that so vauntingly swore
That the havoc of war & the battle's confusion
A home & a country should leave us no more?
Their blood has wash'd out their foul footstep's pollution
No refuge could save the hireling & slave,
From the terror of flight or the gloom of the grave.
And the star-spangled banner in triumph doth wave
O'er the land of the free & the home of the brave.

O! thus be it ever when freemen shall stand
Between their lov'd homes & the war's desolation.
Blest with vict'ry & peace, may the heav'n rescued land
Praise the power that hath made & preserv'd us a nation.
Then conquer we must—when our cause it is just,
And this be our motto—In God is our trust.
And the star-spangled banner in triumph shall wave
O'er the land of the free and the home of the brave.

F S Key

Washington
Oct 21 — 40.

These are the words to "The Star-Spangled Banner" in Francis Scott Key's handwriting.

The United States had just proved—for the second time—that the young nation could stand up to Britain. Britain may have been the greatest military power in the world, but the U.S. was strong enough to stand alone. After the War of 1812, Britain began to think of the U.S. as a real, independent country. Many other nations in the world also saw the U.S. in a new light.

Over the next 100 years, the song grew in popularity. In 1889 the secretary of the navy gave an order. He said that the song should be played at morning flag-raising ceremonies. By the end of World War I, both the army and the navy used the song as if it were the national anthem. In fact, President Wilson named it the national anthem in 1916. In 1931 Congress confirmed the order, which made it official.

What became of the flag itself? Armistead kept it. He was the person who had ordered the flag made. He was also the one who had been in charge of Fort McHenry when the battle was fought. When Armistead died in 1818, he left the flag to his wife. In 1861 it was passed to his daughter, Georgiana Armistead Appleton. Georgiana inherited the flag for two reasons. She had been born at Fort McHenry, and she was named after her father.

Georgiana lent the flag out for patriotic ceremonies. By 1876 she had come to feel that the flag should be given to a museum. However, she died in 1878 before deciding what to do with the flag.

After "The Star-Spangled Banner" became the national anthem in 1916, many people bought the sheet music to the song.

The flag then passed to Eben Appleton, the grandson of Colonel Armistead. Appleton lent the flag to the Smithsonian Institution in Washington, D.C. In 1912 he made the flag a permanent gift.

When the flag arrived at the museum, it was almost a century old. It was in tatters. In the first place, the flag was much smaller than it had been in 1814. By 1912 it had lost eight feet (2 m) of its length. It measured about 30 feet (9 m) by 34 feet (10 m).

Pieces of the flag had been given away. Georgiana Appleton wrote that over the years, many people had asked for pieces of the famous flag. She and her mother had snipped off pieces to give away. One of the 15 stars had even been cut out and given away.

The flag had other holes as well. Many people thought the holes might be battle scars. That's what many people think. A flag that flew during a fierce battle would surely have some holes shot through it. But the answer may not be so simple.

Historians are not sure if the huge flag was flying during the battle. You may remember that Mary Pickersgill made two flags for Fort McHenry. There was the giant banner and the smaller storm flag. The night of the battle was rainy. Some historians believe that the storm flag must have been flying during the fighting. Some think that both flags were raised at different times during the battle.

One thing is certain: The giant flag was flying over the fort the morning after the battle. When Key looked at the fort, that was the flag he saw. It was the flag that inspired his poem. It was the "The Star-Spangled Banner."

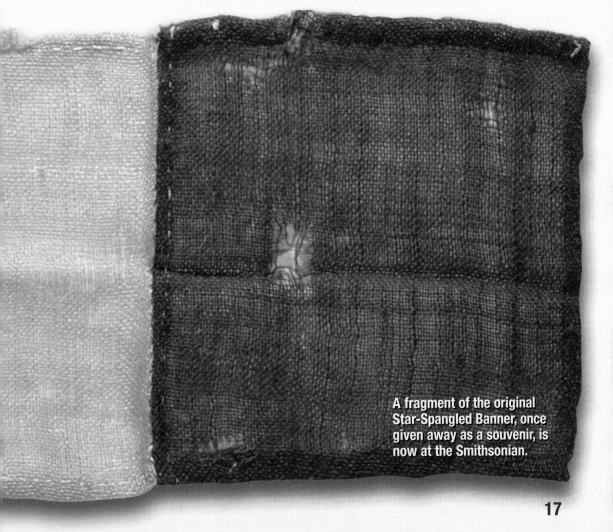

A fragment of the original Star-Spangled Banner, once given away as a souvenir, is now at the Smithsonian.

Of course, the people at the museum were thrilled to be given the famous flag. However, they knew it needed special care. The flag was made of wool and cotton. When it was flown for a year at Fort McHenry, the fabric had been weakened. Light had faded the flag. Some of the wool had even been damaged by insects over the years. It was important to take steps to protect the flag from further damage.

In 1873 a layer of sailcloth had been lightly stitched to the flag to give it support while it was being photographed. The sailcloth was heavy and it was not attached evenly. It tugged at the flag. Now the backing had to be removed because it didn't give the flag enough support for it to be displayed.

In 1914 the Smithsonian hired a flag restorer named Amelia Fowler to work on the flag. Fowler brought in a team of needleworkers. They stitched the flag to a linen backing. They had to attach the linen in a way that would give the flag even support.

The restorers covered the whole flag with a thread mesh. About 1.7 million stitches were used to attach the flag to the linen backing. The thread was dyed the same color as the different parts of the flag.

The flag was folded carefully and placed in a large glass case in the museum. This allowed visitors to see part of the flag up close. The flag was on display from 1914 until 1963. (It was removed for two years during World War II and stored outside of the nation's capital for safekeeping.)

In the 1960s the Star-Spangled Banner was moved to a new building at the Smithsonian. The flag was placed in the building that is now called the National Museum of American History. Architects designed a special hall for the flag. In the new hall, visitors could see the entire flag.

The area where the flag is now kept is said to be "even cleaner than a hospital."

For 35 years the flag hung in its place of honor in Flag Hall. From time to time, the flag was inspected and cleaned. In 1994 museum officials decided that a new approach was needed to care for the flag.

In December 1998, conservators—professionals trained in the care of historic objects—took the first step. Their plan was to remove the flag from its exhibit place. Just trying to move the flag could damage it badly. So conservators covered the flag front and back to protect it. They supported the flag on a frame. Then they lowered the frame to the floor.

The conservators used a screen to protect the flag while they carefully vacuumed it. Next, workers rolled up the flag. They built a crate around it. Then it was ready to be moved to a laboratory where it would be repaired.

The important flag needed a very special lab. It had to be a big room so that the flag could be laid out flat. The flag was placed on a large work surface. A movable bridge was built to pass over the flag's surface. Up to seven conservators could sit or lie on the bridge at once. In this way, they could work on the flag without damaging it and still reach all areas.

The flag lab is kept at just the right temperature. Equipment controls the level of moisture in the room. Filters keep the air clean. There are no bright lights to damage the fabric.

Amelia Fowler (standing) points to the star signed by Georgiana Appleton.

What about the public? Even though the flag is being preserved, visitors can still see it. One wall of the lab is made of glass. This allows people to watch the staff at work on the famous flag.

What are the conservators doing? Once the flag was safely in the lab, their first job was to examine it. They checked every inch of the flag. They wrote down every detail about its condition. When they were done, they took photos of the whole flag.

The second step was to take off the backing that was sewn on in 1914. That meant carefully snipping more than one million stitches. To cut each stitch a conservator would lift it with tweezers. Then the stitch would be cut with tiny scissors. With all the stitches out, the linen backing could be removed.

The third step is cleaning the Star-Spangled Banner. The purpose is to remove anything that might harm the flag over time. Finally, the conservators will prepare the flag for exhibit. When it is ready for display, the flag will be in a room big enough for visitors to see all of it, a room with a glass wall. The room's temperature, light, and moisture will all be carefully controlled.

Visitors view the conserved flag, which is protected by a glass wall.

Workers use a variety of tools, including surgical instruments, to carefully remove the backing attached to the flag in 1914.

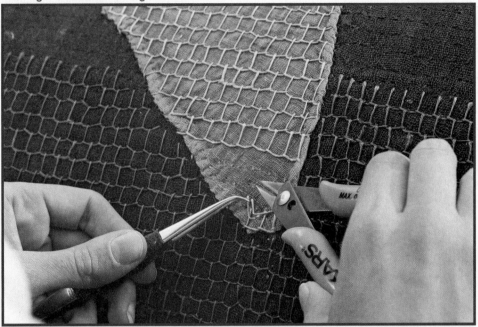

HOW TO TREAT THE U.S. FLAG Special rules about the care of the U.S. flag have been established. The rules tell how to treat the flag with respect. These are some of them:

The flag should only be shown during daylight. If it is flown at night, it should be lit up.

Only a special, all-weather flag may be flown during rain or snow.

The flag should never touch anything beneath it, such as the ground, the floor, water, or merchandise.

The flag should never be carried flat. It should be held aloft and free.

The flag should never be used as a covering for a ceiling.

The flag should never be used to advertise a product.

When the flag is no longer in good condition, it should be retired with respect by designated groups like the Boy Scouts of America or the American Legion.

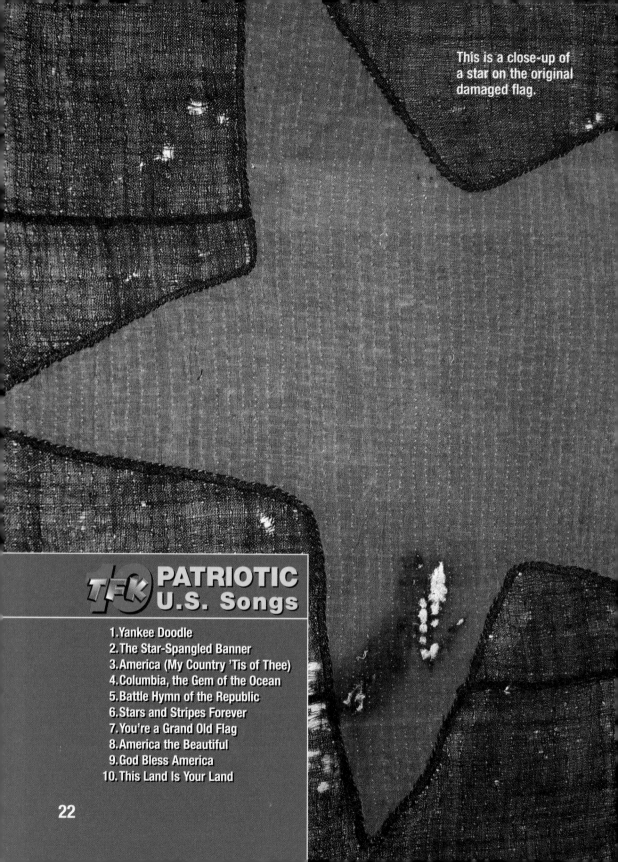

This is a close-up of a star on the original damaged flag.

10 TFK PATRIOTIC U.S. Songs

There's a good chance that Francis Scott Key would understand very well the importance of this flag. Think about his poem. His words came from the heart. They spoke of his love for his country. They spoke of his pride. Key knew that he was not alone. Many people shared his feelings. His song was popular because so many people felt as he did. The song helped Americans think about the meaning of the flag and how it is a symbol of their country. Key wrote in his poem, "our flag was still there." He meant that the United States was "still there," too.

Key's song connected feelings of patriotism to the flag. When people see the flag now, they think of Key's words. They feel proud of their country. Many people feel that it is important to show respect for the flag. That is a way to show respect for the country.

So Francis Scott Key did much more than simply write a poem about a flag. He created a national anthem. He also gave the people of the U.S. a new way to think about their flag and their nation.

Think back to the story of the Battle of Fort McHenry. Think about what Key was feeling when he wrote his poem.

His poem has four verses. The most popular verse is the first. It sums up the story of the battle.

The two middle parts have some angry comments about Britain. Remember that Britain and the United States were at war. That was a long time ago. For many years, Britain and the U.S. have been good friends. So the two middle parts are not usually sung anymore.

Some people like to sing the fourth verse after they sing the first. The whole poem is on page 24. Read the words and imagine what Key felt and saw.

The Star-Spangled Banner

Oh, say can you see by the dawn's early light
What so proudly we hail'd at the twilight's last gleaming,
Whose broad stripes and bright stars through the perilous fight
O'er the ramparts we watch'd were so gallantly streaming?
And the rockets' red glare, the bombs bursting in air,
Gave proof through the night that our flag was still there.
Oh, say does that star-spangled banner yet wave
O'er the land of the free and the home of the brave?

On the shore dimly seen through the mists of the deep,
Where the foe's haughty host in dread silence reposes,
What is that which the breeze, o'er the towering steep,
As it fitfully blows, half conceals, half discloses?
Now it catches the gleam of the morning's first beam,
In full glory reflected now shines on the stream.
'Tis the star-spangled banner, oh, long may it wave
O'er the land of the free and the home of the brave!

And where is that band who so vauntingly swore
That the havoc of war and the battle's confusion
A home and a country should leave us no more?
Their blood has wash'd out their foul footstep's pollution.
No refuge could save the hireling and slave
From the terror of flight or the gloom of the grave,
And the star-spangled banner in triumph doth wave
O'er the land of the free and the home of the brave.

Oh, thus be it ever when freemen shall stand
Between their lov'd home and the war's desolation!
Blest with vict'ry and peace may the heav'n-rescued land
Praise the power that hath made and preserv'd us a nation!
Then conquer we must, when our cause it is just,
And this be our motto, "In God is our Trust,"
And the star-spangled banner in triumph shall wave
O'er the land of the free and the home of the brave.

Visitors to the Smithsonian were once able to see the hanging flag. Now they must view it in a laboratory at the museum.